The Rocky Island

A VICTORIAN CLASSIC FOR CHILDREN

The Rocky Island

and Other Stories

Compiled, revised and updated by
Christopher Wright

BRIDGE PUBLISHING, INC.

Publishers of
LOGOS • HAVEN • OPEN SCROLL

Other children's classics
revised and updated by
Christopher Wright:

Christiana's Journey by John Bunyan
Young Christian's Pilgrimage by John Bunyan
Target Earth! by John Bunyan
Christie's Old Organ by Mrs. O.F. Walton
A Peep Behind the Scenes by Mrs. O.F. Walton

The Rocky Island and Other Stories
Copyright © 1982 this revised edition by Christopher Wright
All rights reserved
Printed in the United States of America
Library of Congress Catalog Card Number: 82-74324
International Standard Book Number: 0-88270-543-1
Bridge Publishing, Inc., South Plainfield, New Jersey 07080

Contents

A LESSON OF FAITH

by Margaret Gatty

"Let me hire you as a nurse for my poor children," said a butterfly to a caterpillar who was strolling along the leaf of a large nettle in her odd, lumbering way.

"See these little eggs?" continued the butterfly. "I don't know how long it will be before they come to life, and I feel very sick and poorly. If I should die, who will take care of my tiny butterflies when I am gone? Will *you,* kind caterpillar? But you must be careful what you give them to eat—they cannot, of course, live on *your* rough food!

"You must give them early dew, and honey from flowers. And you must let them fly, but only a little way at first—for, of course, one can't expect them to use their wings properly all at once. Dear me, what a sad pity it is that you cannot fly yourself. But I have no time to look for another nurse now, so you will do your best, I hope."

The butterfly shook her head. "Dear! dear! I cannot think what made me come and lay my eggs on a stinging nettle! What a place for young butterflies to be born upon! And to think how many beautiful plants and blossoms I have visited this glorious springtime! Still, you will be kind to my poor little ones, will you

1

not? Here, take this red dust from my wings as a reward. Oh, how dizzy I am! Caterpillar, you will remember about the food—"

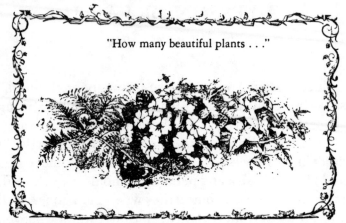

"How many beautiful plants . . ."

With these words, the butterfly drooped her wings and died. The caterpillar, who had not had the opportunity to even say yes or no to the request, was left standing alone by the side of the butterfly's eggs.

"A pretty nurse she has chosen indeed, poor lady!" exclaimed the caterpillar. "And a pretty business I have in hand! Why, her senses must have left her, or she never would have asked a poor, crawling creature like me to bring up her dainty, little ones! Much notice they'll take of me, truly, when they discover the wings on their backs, and fly away out of my sight whenever they choose! Ah, how silly some people are, in spite of their painted clothes and the beautiful dust on their wings!"

However, the poor butterfly was dead, and there lay

the eggs on the nettle leaf. The caterpillar had a kind heart, so she resolved to do her best. But she got no sleep that night, for she was very anxious. She made her back ache from walking all night around her young charges, for fear any harm should happen to them. In the morning she said to herself, "Two heads are better than one. I will consult some wise animal upon the matter and get advice. How should a poor, crawling creature like me know what to do without asking my betters?"

But still there was a difficulty—whom should the caterpillar consult? There was the shaggy dog who sometimes came into the garden. But he was so rough! He would most likely whisk all the eggs off the nettle with one brush of his tail, if she called him near to talk to her, and then she should never forgive herself. There was the tomcat, to be sure, who would sometimes sit at the foot of the apple tree, basking himself and warming his fur in the sunshine. But there was no hope of his troubling himself to think about *butterflies'* eggs!

"I wonder which is the wisest of all the animals I know," sighed the caterpillar, in great distress. And then she thought, and thought, till at last she thought of the robin. She imagined that because he went from place to place and was *very* inquisitive, he must be very clever, and know a great deal. To fly through the air (which *she* could never do) was the caterpillar's idea of perfect glory.

Now, in the neighboring garden there lived a robin,

and the caterpillar sent a message to him to beg him to come and talk to her. When he came she told him all her difficulties, and asked him how to feed and rear the little creatures so different from herself.

"Perhaps you will be able to inquire and hear something about it next time you fly about," observed the caterpillar timidly.

The robin said perhaps he should, and soon afterwards went singing away into the bright, blue sky. By degrees his voice died away in the distance, till the caterpillar could not hear a sound. Even when she reared herself up most carefully, which she did now, she could neither see nor hear the robin.

She dropped upon her legs again, and resumed her walk round the butterfly's eggs, nibbling a bit of one nettle leaf as she moved along.

"What a long time the robin has been gone!" she cried at last. "I wonder where he is now? I would give all my legs to know! He must have flown far away this time. How I would like to know where he goes to, and what he hears in that curious, blue sky!"

And the caterpillar took another turn round the butterfly's eggs.

At last the robin's voice could be heard again. The caterpillar almost jumped for joy, and it was not long before she saw her friend descend to the nettle bed.

"News, news, glorious news, friend caterpillar!" sang the robin. "But the worst of it is, you won't believe me!"

"I believe everything I am told," observed the

"But the worst of it is, you won't believe me!"

caterpillar hastily.

"Well, then, first of all, I will tell you what these little creatures need to eat." And the robin nodded his beak towards the eggs. "What do you think it is? Guess!"

"Dew, and the honey out of flowers, I am afraid," sighed the caterpillar.

"No such thing, old lady! Something simpler than that. Something that *you* can get easily."

"I can get at nothing easily but nettle leaves," murmured the caterpillar in distress.

"Excellent, my good friend!" cried the robin. "You have found it out. You are to feed them with the leaves of nettles!"

"Never!" said the caterpillar, indignantly. "It was

their dying mother's last request that I should do no such thing."

"Their dying mother knew nothing about the matter," persisted the robin. "But why do you ask me, and then disbelieve what I say? You have neither faith nor trust."

"Oh, I believe *everything* I am told," said the caterpillar.

"No, you do not," replied the robin. "You won't believe me about the food, and yet that is only the beginning of what I have to tell you. Why, caterpillar, what do you think those little eggs will turn out to be?"

"Butterflies, to be sure," said the caterpillar.

"Caterpillars!" chirped the robin. "And you'll find it out in time." And he flew away, for he did not want to stay and argue with his friend.

"I thought the robin would be wise and kind," observed the caterpillar, once more beginning to walk round the eggs. "But I find he is foolish and insulting instead. Perhaps he flew *too* far this time. Ah, it's a pity when people who fly so high are silly and rude nevertheless! I still wonder who he sees, and what he does up yonder."

"I would tell you, if you would believe me," sang the robin, descending once more.

"I believe everything I am told," repeated the caterpillar, with as solemn a face as if it were a fact.

"Then I'll tell you something else," cried the robin, "for the best news remains. *One day, you will be a butterfly yourself!"*

"Wretched bird!" exclaimed the caterpillar. "You jest with my inferiority—now you are cruel as well as foolish. Go away! I will ask your advice no more!"

"I told you you would not believe me," cried the robin, sounding angry.

"I believe *everything* that I am told," persisted the caterpillar. "That is"—and she hesitated—"everything that it is *reasonable* to believe. But to tell me that butterflies' eggs are caterpillars, and that caterpillars stop crawling and grow wings and become butterflies! Robin, you are too wise to believe such nonsense yourself, for you *know* it is impossible!"

"I know no such thing," said the robin. "Whether I hover over the gardens, or go high up into the sky, I see so many wonderful things. I know no reason why there should not be more. Oh, caterpillar, it is only because you crawl, because you never get beyond your patch of nettles, that you call these things *impossible*."

"Nonsense!" shouted the caterpillar. "I know what's possible and what's not possible, according to my experience and capacity, as well as you do. Look at my long body and these endless legs, and then talk to me about having wings! You *foolish* bird!"

"And you are a foolish caterpillar!" cried the indignant robin. "You are foolish to attempt to reason about what you cannot understand! Do you not hear how my song swells with rejoicing when I have visited the mysterious wonderworld above? Oh, caterpillar, what you hear from one who has been there and returned, receive with trust."

"That is what you call—"

"Faith," interrupted the robin.

"How am I to learn faith?" asked the caterpillar.

At that moment she felt something at her side. She looked round. Eight or ten dark, little caterpillars were moving about and had already made a hole in the leaf of the tall nettle. They had broken from the butterfly's eggs!

Shame and amazement filled the caterpillar's heart, but joy soon followed. For, as the first wonder was possible, the second might be so too. Perhaps she *would* become a butterfly!

"Teach me your lesson, robin!" she said, and the robin sang to her of the wonders of the earth below, and of the heaven above. And the caterpillar talked all the rest of her life to her relatives of the time when she shall be a butterfly.

But none of them believed her. Nevertheless she had learned the robin's lesson of faith and, when she was going into her chrysalis, she said, "I shall be a butterfly some day!"

But her relatives thought her head was wandering, and they said, "Poor thing!"

But as the chrysalis sealed around her, the caterpillar said quietly, "I have known many wonders. I have faith—I can trust even now for what shall come next!"

THE KING AND HIS SERVANTS

by Samuel Wilberforce

A great king once called his servants to him, and said, "Many times you have told me that you love me and that you wish to serve me. I have never put you to the test. The time has now come to find those who really want to serve me, to discover who really means what they say. The test I am giving you will start tomorrow. Prepare yourselves for a long journey. I will tell you all you need to know when you meet here in the morning."

When he had said this, the king dismissed his servants. As soon as they left, they began to talk to each other in great excitement. Some got busy with their preparations straight away. They told the others they hoped the test would be a difficult one because they wanted to show the king just how much they cared for him.

Others were very quiet and sat thinking about the next day, wondering if they would be good enough to do well in the test the king had planned.

Whatever their preparations for the next day, all these servants had a very good reason to want to please the king: The king had sent his son to rescue them from a cruel and wicked enemy. The enemy had kept them in dungeons and made them work for him. But all that was in the past. The good king and his son had beaten this enemy, and had taken the servants all back to live in his palace. These servants had been promised crowns and thrones and much more by the king. It was no surprise, therefore, that they all said they would be ready for any test the good king might set before them.

Not all the servants were brave, but the ones who felt most afraid remembered promises made by the king. They remembered that he had said he would give them all the strength they needed day by day. They remembered also how kind and loving the king had been to rescue them from the enemy. So, even though they were afraid that they might fail their king, these servants joined with the bolder, less fearful ones as they made ready for the great test.

Many worked till late into the night. The king warned them that the journey would be long, and there were so many things to do in preparation.

The servants remembered that long ago the king told them there would be a test and even gave them instructions. These instructions now had to be used for the journey. In the morning there would be so much rush and excitement, they might forget to take them!

Early the next day everyone went to the palace court to meet their king. The king greeted the servants from his palace door as they waited in excitement to hear what the test was to be.

"I have opened my treasure houses," said the king as the servants listened carefully. "You will see that I have brought out gold and silver, and many precious things. These are being lent to you, but I want you to think of them as gifts. Far away from my palace there is a great city. In that city there are many merchants. I want you to take these gifts to the city, and trade in the marketplace. You must use your gifts wisely. When the time comes for you to return to me, I want you to come back with many wonderful things."

The servants became very excited when they heard this. The gifts were marvelous indeed. To use them to trade in the far city was something they all wanted to do for their king. Of all tests, surely this must be the most exciting imaginable!

The king saw the joy on his servants' faces. Then he held his hand up as though to warn them. "In that city," said the king solemnly, "there are people who are not your friends. They will try to rob you of your gifts. They will try to make you waste your time but you must always remember that you will have to come back to me, and I shall want to see how well you have used your gifts."

The servants held onto their treasures tightly when they heard this. No one was going to steal from *them* or make *them* waste these precious gifts.

The king then explained that early morning was the best time for trading in the market of that city. All the finest goods would be on sale in the early morning. The precious stones and jewels would be the best in the city. Later in the day all these goods would be gone.

"At the end of the day," warned the king, "there will

be the sound of a trumpet. That trumpet call will summon you all back home."

Several of the servants looked at each other in alarm when they heard this. To hear the trumpet call and be empty-handed would be a disgrace indeed. To come back with nothing to offer the king was unthinkable. Slowly the servants packed their bags.

The journey would be a long and hard one across vast deserts. No sand must get into the precious bundles to harm the goods. However, only some of the servants packed carefully enough to be sure that all their gifts would be easy to reach when they arrived at the great city. There were only a few who seemed to remember that the king had said the best time to begin their trade was in the early morning.

Other servants laughed at the careful ones. "There will be time enough when we get there," they said.

But when the journey was over, and they all arrived at the city gates, these same servants decided to leave their unpacking until the next morning. "The journey has been long and hot and difficult," they complained. "We need to rest first, and plenty to eat and drink." So they stayed up late, enjoying themselves and quite forgetting the king's advice.

As the sun rose the next day, most of the servants jumped up and began to get ready. They talked excitedly of what lay before them that day as they traded for their king. The servants who had stayed up until late turned in their sleep and complained at all the noise. But the ones who had been careful to do

They all arrived at the city gates.

exactly as the king had told them took no notice, and marched into the city with their goods packed on their backs.

What a great city it was! How many people lived there they had no idea. There were houses and streets in all directions. Most of the inhabitants must still be asleep, for the servants walked along the streets unimpeded, in spite of the large packs on their backs. The few people from the city who were walking on the streets were going in the same direction they were. In the marketplace, there was plenty of room for the king's servants to display their precious wares.

The merchants from the city came round to see what they had to offer. Then, in return, they showed what goods they had.

It was just as the king had said. The servants were given first choice of all that the merchants had to offer. There were rubies and diamonds and pearls such as they had never seen before for size and beauty. One large pearl was so precious it was called a pearl of great price. They bought this for their king, while others continued to trade with the merchants of the city until they had more treasure than they had come with.

Some of the servants were more clever than their fellows at trading, but each servant made the best use he could of his skills. The pearl of great price was the most cherished possession of some. Others had bought beautiful robes adorned with gold and jewels. Still others had spices from Arabia, or precious perfume from the islands of the East.

One of these servants seemed to have nothing to carry home with him. Yet, like the others, he had treasure in his pack. One of his friends asked him what he had done with his gifts.

"I have no riches which I can show you," said the servant. "But in my pack I have an offering which I know the king will treasure because of his mercy and kindness."

The others gathered round and begged him to tell his story.

"I was walking through the market," said the servant, "when I saw a poor woman standing all alone and crying to herself. I asked her why she was so sad. I thought her heart would break as she told me how her husband had borrowed large sums of money from some men, and now he was dead. The men heard of his death and came round to demand their money back. But the money had been spent long ago, so the men forced their way into the house and took all that she had. They took her children too, and were going to sell them as slaves so they could get their money back."

The other servants listened, grim faced at the thought of such heartless men.

"You will not wonder that I opened my pack of treasure and offered to repay the debt. There was only just a sufficient amount to pay back the money that was owed and to set the children free and let the woman live in peace." The merchant showed the others what was now in his pack. "I have no treasure of precious stones to take back to our king. All I have is the woman's tears and thankfulness. I am sure the king will be pleased with what I bring."

The other servants told him that this was surely one of the best gifts with which any of them could return. They continued with their trading, as they thought of how much their king must love them. They remembered the times during which they had been prisoners in the enemy's dungeons, and when the king's son had come to rescue them. Their hearts were filled with gratefulness, and they were all glad to be taking precious gifts back to their king.

How excited they would all be when the trumpet sounded. They knew not when that trumpet would sound but, whenever it did sound loud and clear, they *knew* they would be going home to meet their king.

The sun was now high in the sky, and the city was becoming busy. How different from the early morning when the streets were nearly deserted. People were now pouring out of their houses—some for work, others just to enjoy themselves and still others were coming to do nothing but watch the people passing by.

The servants were indeed glad they had set about their trading early. By now, the merchants had closed up their richest stores and were replaced by men with imitation pearls and fake jewellery. There appeared to be hardly any honest traders left in the marketplace. Noisy people pushed their way through the crowds, and men called out to announce traveling sideshows. In the shadows, at the edge of the marketplace, men lay in wait to see who they could catch and rob.

The king's servants observed all these things. Some of the things they saw were good to look at, and some of the music was indeed pleasant to listen to. There were bands of musicians and singers walking up and down through the market. The servants enjoyed it all, but always remembered the king and his son—their prince. Even when the surrounding lights were at their brightest and the music was at its sweetest, these servants were always listening for the trumpet that would call them home. They did not want to be ashamed of what they were doing when the call came for them to return.

If only this had been so with *all* the king's servants! When these first servants had set out early the others, who had stayed up late the night before, turned over and began to complain about the noise. True, some *nearly* got up to join the early risers, but their goods had not been prepared for trading. So they decided that it might be as well to wait until all the other servants were up, and then go to the market. They did not intend to be late but they saw no reason why they should be so very early.

They slept, therefore, until the sun was high, and then rose in a rush because it was now so late. All their goods had to be unpacked and sorted, and the dust of the journey had to be shaken off. These servants were secretly angry with themselves but began to pick on each other. They accused the others for making them late, and they argued so fiercely that they slowed each other down. Instead of making the best use of what time remained, they made themselves more and more late.

In the end, after many harsh words and much bad temper, they finally got on their way. Some still had their goods in a muddle, but off they went—each making his own way to the market—when they could have helped each other to find the way.

As soon as they entered the city gates, these slothful servants found so many people pushing and pulling this way and that, that they thought they would never get to the marketplace. People began to laugh at the way they were dressed, and as soon as they opened their packs to begin trading, children gathered round and made fun of them. There seemed to be no way these servants could trade their precious gifts.

Some, who had boasted loudly that they hoped the test would be a hard one, were now the first to give up when the crowd made things difficult for them. They packed up their goods and joined in with the throng. It was difficult to tell them apart. On and on the great multitude pushed its way to a place where there was a large show tent. Men stood outside and blew trumpets, while others shouted invitations to all to come and see the strange sights which were within.

One of the servants stood watching as the people of the city swarmed inside. In the end he too went to the entrance. The showman asked for his money but when he saw that the coins belonged to another country he turned the servant away.

"Stand back!" he cried.

But, as the servant walked away, the showman saw the pack of precious gifts. At this he changed his tone. "My friend, do not go," he called. "Give me your pack of goods, and I will let you in!"

For a moment the servant stopped. He thought of the king, and how he had told all the servants to use their gifts wisely. Then he almost made up his mind to make his way back to the marketplace and trade for his lord, cost him what it might. But at that moment there was a great burst of the showman's trumpets, and he heard the shouts of excitement from inside the tent. Quickly, he forgot his instructions, and as fast as he could slip his pack from his shoulders and hand it to the showman, the servant was inside.

Another of the king's servants was standing at the corner of a street watching some jugglers. He was so captivated that he forgot all about trading for his master and thought of nothing but the jugglers. As he watched so intently, some evil-minded men crept up behind him and, without his knowing, stole all the gold from his pack. The servant continued to stare at the show. When he came to trade for his master, he would discover his loss. And when the trumpet sounded he would have nothing to take back for his Lord.

Other servants were treated worse than this one was. One of them followed the shows and crowds from street to street until he came to the very edge of the city. Over some fields he fancied he saw even more exciting sights. No sooner did he set out, than some robbers rushed from a hiding place and beat him up.

19

Standing . . . watching some jugglers.

With his goods gone he hardly had the strength to get back to the city.

Another of these lazy servants suddenly became very afraid as he watched the crowds. One of his friends asked him why he trembled. At first he could not answer, but after a while he explained that he had just heard one of the showmen's trumpets, and it reminded him of his master's great trumpet sound, which was yet to come. He had become afraid because much of the day had gone already, and he had not even begun to trade for his Lord.

"How shall we stand before our king with our hands empty?" he asked his friends.

Some of his lazy companions laughed at him for this. But this servant's fears were wiser than their laughter.

"You are in the same danger," he said sadly. "How then can you jeer at me?" He pointed up toward the sky and showed them how low the sun was getting. At any moment, the trumpet might sound and they would have nothing to take back to their Lord.

As this servant spoke, one of his friends listened eagerly to him. "What can we do?" he asked. "Have we left it too late?"

"It is never too late, until the trumpet sounds," said the other. "Even though we have wasted most of the day, perhaps there is something we can do. Come with me to the marketplace, and we will see."

So the second servant agreed. Off they set, pushing their way past old friends, who began shouting at them and making fun. The commotion made the crowds of the city join in. How hard it was now for these two servants, and how they wished they had set out early to the market to trade their gifts for their king. The people in the crowd were rude to them, and at times angry. Whenever they met some of the lazy servants, these began to turn yet more of the crowd against them.

"Do you think we shall ever get there?" asked the servant who had been persuaded to come by his friend. Pushing against the throng coming their way was like swimming against the current in a swiftly moving stream. "Do you think we shall ever get there?"

"Yes, yes!" cried the other. "We shall get there."

His companion was not so sure. "It is so hard to keep going. The streets seem to get more and more full. I am afraid we shall never get through."

Just as he spoke, a great band of the townspeople met them like a mighty wave. There was music and trumpets and dancing, and all this seemed sure to drive the two servants back. One of their old friends was dancing among the rest. He was the man who had given away his pack of treasures to go into the showman's tent. Now, as soon as he saw the two servants, he called to them by their names and invited them to join with the crowd.

The servant who was leading the way shook his head. "No, we will not join with you. We are going to the marketplace to trade for our Lord."

"It is too late. You should have done that in the morning. There is no point in going on now."

This servant, who had been so afraid earlier, now turned very pale, but still he kept on his way. "Yes," he called. "We have wasted the morning, and that makes me very sad. But our good Lord will help us even now, and we *will* serve him."

Then the servant who was with the crowd turned to the servant's companion. "How about you? Won't you join us in our fun? Your friend is going mad. What is the use of going to the market when it is closed?"

Then the second servant hung his head in shame. He would have given up and joined with the crowd if his friend had not seized him by the hand and told him to keep going and to think of his kind master and his master's son—whose very blood had been shed for them. With that, the second servant seemed to get strength and held onto his friend as they pushed forward.

Then their former companion turned on them in hate. He shouted to the crowd to grab hold of them and stop them. The noisy crowd would have done this if the two servants had not managed to push their way through, using a strength that seemed to come from beyond them. Almost immediately they were in another street.

There were fewer people here, and the two servants paused to recover their breath. But the crowd and its music could still be heard in the distance as the two servants rested.

"I could never have held on through the crowd if you had not helped me," said the second servant.

"It was our master's strength," said his friend.

"Then do you think he will accept what we can get, now that the day is nearly over? I wish I had your courage. I am so afraid that if I meet that crowd again they will tear us in pieces."

"Our king will never let that be," said his friend. "We must trust in him."

Just then the crowd of singers, dancers and musicians came bursting round the corner. Leading them was their former companion again, who had urged them to join him and the crowd. The servant, who had been so frightened before, became even more anxious now.

Close to where the two servants were standing there was a large shop. In the window there shone what appeared to be precious stones and jewels, diamonds, and gold and ivory. The second servant turned quickly to his friend.

"Look in here," he said. "Surely all we need is in this shop. Let us go in and trade for our master. We will also escape from the crowd."

"No, no!" cried his friend. "We must make our way to the marketplace, for that is where our Lord told us to trade. We must not turn aside from the proper way. Being late has brought us troubles, but this shop has nothing good enough to take back for our master. Keep going and we shall soon be in the market."

The second servant held back. "I know that the crowd will tear us to pieces. Look how many people there are! I think that our former companion has seen us, and he is bringing the crowd over."

"Do not be afraid. Our king will keep us safe. Although ten-thousand enemies surround me on every side, I am not afraid."

The second servant seemed not to hear his friend. The shopkeeper had been watching the two men, and now he came out to invite them in.

"Come in, come in," he said. "Be quick, before the crowd sweeps you away. Come in and buy my pearls, and my diamonds, and my precious stones. Come in, come in."

And while the second servant paused to hear what the shopkeeper had to offer, the crowd swept past them and the two servants were separated. The second servant realised his friend had gone and without further thought he hurried into the shop, hoping to be safe there.

Now the shopkeeper seemed to be an honest man but, really, his shining jewels and pearls and diamonds were nothing but coloured glass. They were all absolutely worthless. However, the servant did not know this. If it had been earlier in the day, the clear morning light would have shown the imitation jewellery for what it was. The brightness of the day was fading now, and the red light of the evening sun made the false goods difficult to see clearly.

So the shopkeeper persuaded the servant to part with all his riches and gave him nothing in return but bits of coloured glass. What a poor showing these would make when presented to the king.

The servant had no idea that he had been cheated. Or, if the thought crossed his mind that something might be wrong, he knew that he must now take the blame for his wasted time and gifts. As he left the shop, the servant became unhappy and stared down the road, beginning to wish he had stayed with his friend and pushed on to the marketplace.

And what a hard struggle faced his friend before he finally got there. At times it seemed as if the words of his former companion were going to come true, and he would indeed be torn to pieces. The crowd pressed fiercely against him from all directions. Then, just when it seemed they would never let him pass, something made the people break off their pushing and the servant found a way through. As we went, he continued saying over and over again the words from the Psalm he had repeated to his friend earlier: "Although ten-thousand enemies surround me on every side, I am not afraid."

As he said these words, the angry crowd parted like a stream around a rock, and he went right through without the crowd even noticing him. At last he reached the marketplace. How glad he was to find himself there, but even so his troubles were not over. Many of the market stalls were empty, and at others there were only dealers in imitation jewellery.

The servant looked around anxiously, afraid that the trumpet would sound before he had a chance to purchase anything for his Lord. Now he was more than sorry that he had wasted so much of the day. "What shall I do? How can I trade for my master when I have wasted my time so badly?"

Then he noticed a stall where there were no jewels, no gold or costly silk, no pearls of great price. All that was on the stall was coarse sackcloth and rough garments. Behind these were ashes, and loaves of bitter bread. Some bottles containing tears rested on leaves of bitter herbs. As he gazed at the stall, something seemed to whisper to him, "Go and buy."

So, full of sadness, the servant stepped forward. He knew deep inside that he was not good enough to trade for his master. With trembling hands he bought the roughest sackcloth, and the ashes. Then he picked up a bottle containing the saddest tears. It was his way of saying to the king that he was truly sorry. After trading his gifts for these, the servant stepped back into the marketplace to wait for the trumpet.

Then suddenly it came! Through the evening air came its clear voice, growing louder and louder. The trumpet sound pealed across the sky, and all the great city with its shows and its noise and its excitement melted away to nothing. Immediately the servants found themselves gathered together and standing with their king. Everything had gone except the servants and their belongings.

The king then called them forward so he could see what they had brought. The servants who had risen early and traded their gifts wisely were given crowns of light and much gladness. Each servant had his own personal reward. The man who had bought the poor

The servant stepped forward.

widow's tears and grateful thanks seemed to bring a gift that pleased the king more than many others.

Then the servant who had wasted the day but who had bought the sackcloth and ashes and bottle of tears stepped forth. He came forward slowly, and his offering was indeed poor to look at. The king placed it amongst the heaps of gold and jewels and precious cloth. The servant looked up at the king and said, almost silently, "A broken and a contrite heart you will not ignore."

And as he spoke, the king looked gently at his servant and smiled. "You are a good and faithful servant," he said.

Then, as the king said this, the coarse sackcloth suddenly shone like cloth woven from threads of gold. The ashes sparkled like the finest jewels, while every tear of sadness in the bottle turned to a pearl or ruby more valuable than any the king already possessed.

Finally, the king turned to his careless servants and, as he spoke, they ran to hide. The king ordered them away from his presence, away from the palace where there was peace and life. The servants who had traded their gifts wisely in the great city for their king were invited to live with him in the wonderful light of the palace, while those who had wasted their time were shut outside in the darkness, weeping.

COBWEBS

by Margaret Gatty

Twinette the spider was young, hungry and industrious. "It is time for you to weave yourself a web, my dear," said her mother. "And catch flies for yourself. Only don't weave near me in the corner here. I am old, and stay in the corners; but you are young, and needn't. Besides, you would be in my way. Scramble along the rafters to a little distance off, and spin. But make sure there's nothing there—below you, I mean—before you begin. You won't catch anything to eat if there isn't empty space about you for the flies to fly in."

Twinette was dutiful, and obeyed. She scrambled along the woodwork of the roof of the church—for it was there her mother lived—till she had gone what she thought might be a suitable distance. Then she stopped to look round which, considering she had eight eyes to do it with, was not difficult. But she was not so sure of what might be below.

"I wonder whether mother would say there was nothing below me but empty space for flies to fly in?" said she.

So she went back to her mother, and asked what she thought.

"Oh dear, oh dear!" said her mother. "How can I

think about what I don't see? There didn't used to be anything there in *my* younger days, I'm sure. But everybody must find out for themselves. Let yourself down by your web and see for yourself if there's anything there or not."

Twinette was a very intelligent young spider. She thanked her mother for this advice and was just starting afresh when another thought struck her. "How shall I know if there's anything there when I get there?" asked she.

"Dear me, if there's anything there, how can you help but see it?" cried the mother, rather vexed by her daughter's inquiring spirit. "You, with at least eight eyes in your head!"

"Thank you. Now I quite understand," said Twinette. Then, scuttling back to the end of the rafter, she began to prepare her long line of web.

It was the most exquisite thing in the world—so fine, you could scarcely see it; so elastic, it could be blown about without breaking; such a perfect grey that it looked white against black things, and black against white; so manageable that Twinette could both make it, and slide down by it at once; and when she wished to get back she could slip up it and roll it up at the same time!

It was a wonderful rope for *anybody* to make. But Twinette was not conceited. Rope-making came naturally to her.

Twinette was about halfway down to the stone-flagged floor when she stopped to rest and look round.

Then, balancing herself at the end of her rope, with her legs crumpled up round her, she spoke to herself.

"This is charming! And it's all so nice in the middle here. Nice empty space for the flies to fly about it; and a very pleasant time they must have of it! Dear me, how hungry I feel. I must go back and weave my web at once."

But just as she was preparing to roll up the rope and be off, a ray of sunshine, streaming through one of the windows, struck in a direct line upon her suspended body—startling her with its dazzling brightness. Everything seemed in a blaze around her, and she turned round and round in terror.

"Oh dear, oh dear, oh dear!" she cried, for she didn't know what else to say and couldn't help calling out. Then, making a great effort, she gave one hearty spring, and, blinded though she was, shot up to the roof as fast as a spider could go, rolling the rope into a ball as she went; after which she stopped to complain.

But it was dull work complaining to herself, so she soon ran back to her mother in the corner.

"Back again so soon, my dear?" asked the old lady, not overpleased at the fresh disturbance.

"That I am back again at all is the wonder!" whimpered Twinette. "There's something down there, after all!"

"Why, what did you see?" asked her mother.

"Nothing; that was just it," answered Twinette. "I could see nothing for dazzle and blaze; but I *did* see dazzle and blaze!"

"Young people today are very troublesome with their observations," remarked the mother. "However, if one rule will not do, here is another. Did this dazzle and blaze push you out of your place, my dear?"

Twinette said, "Certainly not—I came away of myself."

"Then how could they *be* anything?" asked her mother. "Two things could not be in one place at the same time."

Twinette sat very silent, wondering what dazzle and blaze could be if they were nothing at all! This was a question which might have puzzled her forever. But fortunately her mother interrupted by advising her to go and do something. She really couldn't afford to feed her out of *her* web any longer, she said.

"If dazzle and blaze kill me, you'll be sorry, mother," complained Twinette.

"Nonsense about dazzle and blaze!" cried the old spider, now thoroughly roused. "All you saw was light."

So Twinette scuttled off in silence; for she dared not ask what light was, though she wanted very much to know.

But she felt too cross to begin to spin a large web. She preferred to search after truth rather than catch dinner, which showed she was no ordinary spider. So she resolved to go down below, in another place, and see if she could find a really empty space.

When she next lowered herself, it was a little further away, and a very satisfactory journey she seemed to make.

"All's safe so far," she said, her good humour returning. "I do believe I've found nothing at last. How fine it is!"

As she spoke, she hung dangling at the end of her long rope, her legs tucked up round her as before, in perfect enjoyment when, suddenly, the door of the church was thrown open. It was a windy evening, and the draught that poured in blew the web, with Twinette at the end of it, backwards and forwards through the air till she turned quite giddy.

"Oh dear, oh dear!" she cried. "What shall I do? How could they say there is nothing here—oh dear! But empty space for flies to fly in?"

At last, in despair, she made an effort of resistance and, in the very teeth of the wind, succeeded in coiling up the rope and so hauled herself back to the rafters.

Twinette scrambled back to her mother and told her what she thought, though not in plain words. For what she thought was that her mother didn't know what she was talking about when she talked about empty space with nothing in it.

"Dazzle and blaze were nothing," she cried at last, "though they blinded me because we were all in one place together, which we couldn't be if they'd been *anything!* And now this is nothing because I can't see it, though it blows me out of my place twenty times in a minute. What's the use of beliefs one can't depend on, mother? I don't believe you know a *quarter* of what's down below there!"

The old spider's head turned giddy with Twinette's

arguments, just as Twinette's head had done while she was swinging in the wind.

"I don't see that it can matter what's there," she grumbled, "as long as there's room for flies to fly about in. I wish you'd go back and spin!"

But Twinette dawdled and thought, and thought and dawdled, till the day was nearly over.

"I will take one more turn down below," said she to herself at last, "and look round me again."

And so she did, but went further down than before. Then she stopped to rest, as usual. Presently, as she hung—dangling in the air by her line—she grew venturesome. "I will find the end of it all," she thought. "I will see how far empty space goes." So saying, she continued spinning her long line of rope.

It was a wonderful rope, certainly, or it would not have gone on to such a length without breaking. In a few minutes Twinette was on the cold stone floor. But she didn't like the feel of it at all, so she began to run as fast as she could and luckily met with a step of woodwork on one side.

She hurried up this at once, and crept into a corner close by, where she stopped to take a breath.

"One doesn't know what to expect in such queer, outlandish places," she observed. "When I've rested I'll go back, but I must wait till I can see a little better."

But seeing a little better was out of the question, for night was coming on. So, when she became weary of waiting, Twinette stepped out of her hiding place to look round. The whole church was in darkness!

Now it is one thing for a spider to be snug in bed when it is dark, and quite another to be a long way from home and to have lost your way, and not know what may happen to you next minute. Twinette had often been in the dark corner with her mother, and thought nothing of it. But now she shook all over with fright and wondered what dreadful thing this darkness could be.

Then she thought of her mother's ideas, and became angry.

"I can't *see* anything, and I don't *feel* anything," she murmured. "And yet here's *something* that frightens me out of my wits."

At last her very fright made her bold. She felt about for her line of rope. It was there safe and sound, and she made a spring for it. Roll went the rope, and up went its owner; higher, higher, higher through the dark night air—seeing nothing, hearing nothing, feeling nothing but the desperate fear within. By the time she touched the rafter she was exhausted, and as soon as she was safely upon it she fell asleep.

It must have been late next morning when she woke, for the sound of organ music was pealing through the church. The air vibrations swept pleasantly over her body. Rising and falling like gusts of night, the music was swelling and sinking like waves of the sea, gathering and dispersing like vapours of the sky.

Twinette went down by her line to observe, but could see nothing which would account for her sensations. Fresh ones, however, stole round her as she hung suspended, for it was a harvest festival, and large, white lilies were grouped with evergreens round the pillars. They filled the air with their powerful perfume. Yet nothing disturbed Twinette from her place. Sunshine streamed in through the windows—she even felt it warm on her body—but it interfered with nothing else. Meanwhile, in such way as spiders hear, she heard music and prayer. A door opened and a breeze caught her rope. But still, she held fast. So music and prayer and sunshine and breeze and scent were all there together. And Twinette was among them, and saw flies flying about overhead.

This was enough. She went back to the rafter, chose a home, and began to spin. Before evening, her web was completed and her first prey caught and feasted on. Then she cleared the remains out of her chamber and sat down to think. As she crossed and twisted and wove the threads, her ideas grew clearer and clearer. Each line she fastened brought its own reflection, and this was the way they went on: "Empty space is an old wive's tale!" [She fixed that part of the web very tight.] "Sight and touch are very imperfet guides" [this crossed the other at an angle]. "Two or three things can easily be in one place *at the very same time*" [this part seemed very loose till she tightened it by a second line]. "Sunshine and wind and scent and sound don't drive each other out of their places" [that held firm]. "When one has sensations there is something to cause them, whether one sees it, or feels it, or finds it out, or not" [this was a wonderful thread; it went right round the web and was fastened down in several places].

"Light and darkness, and sunshine and wind, and sound and sensation, and fright and pleasure don't keep away flies" [the interlacing threads looked so very strong as she placed them]. "How many things I know of that I don't know much about" [the web got thicker every minute]. "And there may be so many more beyond—ever so many more—beyond."

She kept repeating these words till she finished her web; and when she sat up after supper, to think, she began to repeat them again—for she could think of nothing better or wiser to say. But this was no wonder, for all her thoughts put together made nothing but a cobweb, after all!

And when at last the broom swept the web, with others from the roof, Twinette was no longer there. She had died and bequeathed her cobweb-wisdom to another generation. But it was only cobweb-wisdom after all, for spiders remain spiders still. They weave their webs in the roofs of churches without fathoming the mystery of unseen things on the earth, and the unseen mysteries of heaven that even people cannot understand.

AGATHOS

by *Samuel Wilberforce*

There once was a mighty king, whose country was troubled by a fierce and evil creature. The king called some of his soldiers and sent them to that part of the land where this beast was causing so much trouble.

"I am sending you out to fight with this creature," he told his men. "My son, the prince, has already fought with him. My strength shall go with you in battle. Therefore, be upon your guard. If you remember my words and call upon the name of my son in times of danger, I shall be with you. Above all, take and use this armour which I have provided for you. If you wear it boldly, the enemy can never harm you. But if he finds you unprepared—if he comes upon you when you are without this armour—he will surely slay you!"

The soldiers all promised faithfully to be on their guard. Setting off in high spirits, they soon came to the land where the evil beast lay.

At first, they were all extremely careful to wear their armour. They never all slept at once, but some watched while the others rested. It was a fine sight to see these brave men marching up and down the land, and all the people of the country felt safe and happy because the king's army was keeping guard.

It was splendid to see them early in the morning, when some had been watching while others slept and they were about to change turns. The sleeping men would wake refreshed and, putting their armour on most carefully, they knelt to pray. Earnestly they called upon their prince to keep them loyal. Then they would go out for their turn to keep guard against the evil one.

It was surely a noble sight to see but, alas, it did not last. All the time the soldiers watched, never once did they see the beast. All went on quietly around them. The farmers ploughed their land, the reapers went about to reap the harvest; there were marriages, and feasts, and games and work.

The soldiers began to think that perhaps it was an empty tale that had been spoken of the terrible, evil creature. Soon they forgot their king's instructions to watch and stand fast.

The weather, too, grew very hot and sultry. Their armour seemed heavier than ever before.

"What can be the use of always wearing this heavy helmet?" one of them complained. "The sun heats my armour until it scorches me up!"

"You are right," agreed a friend. "Besides, no one ever sees this enemy. I shall leave *my* helmet in the tent. There will be time enough to run and fetch it when I see him coming!"

Another soldier complained of the weight of his breastplate. Yet another decided that his shield was such a nuisance he would lay it in his tent where he could be sure to reach it in time of danger.

The ground was hot, now. Their thick sandals made the soldiers' feet hot. They grew more and more restless and very tired. Finally, they cast these away and walked barefoot through the sandy ground. It was pleasant to feel the soft earth beneath them.

Before long, the soldiers were walking around the countryside with little of their armour to be seen. Their cool clothes were much more comfortable than those the king had provided, they told each other.

Some went to this feast, while others went to that. It was hard now to tell who belonged to the king, for the men could no longer be identified by their bright armour.

But there was one soldier who would not change his ways. His name was Agathos. He was greatly saddened by the sight of his careless comrades. Often he would remind his friends of the king's warning. He told them that the enemy must surely be near, although they did not see him yet. Had not the prince fought with the evil creature? Surely the king must know how dangerous this enemy could be!

The other soldiers laughed and jeered at Agathos because he would not do as they did. But he accepted their taunts and, at first, neither their harsh words nor the hot sun made him weary. There was nothing they could do to persuade him to put off the armour he had been given by the king. At times his feet were swollen within his heavy sandals. At other times he felt like sleeping when it was his turn to watch at night. But Agathos remembered the king and how he had spoken with words of love. He trusted the king.

As the days and weeks passed, things became more and more difficult for Agathos. The words of the idle soldiers grew harsher. They all—except for Agathos—became more and more certain that the enemy would never attack, if he existed at all.

But just when they thought themselves safe, the danger was suddenly and unexpectedly at hand. One of the soldiers was returning home from a great feast. There had been much merriment, and he had taken off his armour. Now he was walking home in his thin clothing, through the pleasant summer evening air.

The soldier was walking with abandon. He was thinking about the party which had just broken up. He pitied Agathos, who was not able to forget the king for even one moment.

But as these thoughts ran through his mind, he heard a strange, rustling noise in the wood on his right. Instantly—as quick as lightning—the dreadful form of the fierce enemy stood before him.

Terror stricken, the soldier felt for the sharp sword which the king had given to him. It was no longer at his side. There was nothing to help him now. As he turned to run he could see that, all around, the terrible creature had thrown sharp darts which would stick into his unguarded feet. The soldier fell to the ground, and the beast pounced on top of him.

His companions wondered why he did not return home. Two of his closest friends set out to look for him in the darkness. They did not return to the camp. But the other soldiers did not miss them for some time, as they feasted and enjoyed themselves. They neither wore their armour nor remembered the words of the king. They knew nothing of the danger that was at hand.

The evil being had gained courage by this time. He feared the king, but the king's soldiers were not as dangerous as he had imagined they would surely be. He thought that he might even attack the camp itself and destroy all his enemies at once.

For a long time that night the creature lay hiding in the wood which bordered the camp. Agathos was walking up and down, faithfully keeping guard as was his habit. The creature could see the sharp sword hanging at his side and the huge shield with the bright, red cross upon it as it hung over Agathos' shoulder. The wretched fiend remembered his battle with the prince, and he was now afraid of Agathos.

The next day, when noontime had come, Agathos was sleeping in his tent. Other soldiers were on guard, but the enemy had no fear of them. With a mighty, thundering yell he rushed from the cover of the wood and attacked the soldiers tooth and nail. He tore some of them viciously with his cruel hands. He bit others with his sharp teeth, while still others he stung with his poisonous tail.

There was a great shout of alarm throughout the camp for the armour that was so necessary. One soldier managed to reach his sword, and lunged at the dreadful creature. But he had no helmet, and the beastly enemy let his heavy hands crash down upon the man's head.

Another soldier had both his sword and his helmet by this time. He was able to fight longer than the first, and even wounded the enemy in the side. The outraged creature swung round upon the soldier with his tail and, because the man was wearing no armour, the sting penetrated and poisoned his body.

Another man rushed from his tent now; he seemed to be well armed. But in his hurry he had forgotten to pick up his shield which he had earlier thrown carelessly to one side.

This soldier now began to attack the beast bravely. He wounded the creature in the side and in one of its legs. Try as he could, the wretched being could not get a hold on the man. His claws slipped off the helmeted head, and his sting was useless against the soldier's armour.

Suddenly, just as the soldier was pausing to rest, the enemy threw fiery darts out of his evil hands. The sword was no defence against these, and neither was the armour. The shield, left behind in the tent, would have protected the soldier safely.

The next soldier to attack was well prepared with his shield. But because the day was not, he had not fastened the armour upon his body. With his shield knocked aside by the enemy's powerful arms this man, too, fell as the darts struck home. Other soldiers, without sandals on their feet, fell wounded as they trod upon the fiery darts that were strewn upon the ground.

Some soldiers remained in their tents, trembling with fear when they saw the fate of their companions. By now the enemy was triumphing in his great strength. Soon, he thought to himself, he would be able to destroy the king's entire army!

The noise of battle awakened Agathos from his sleep. In a dream he had seen the prince standing before him, his hands and feet deeply wounded. Underneath the prince was the terrible enemy. Both had been wounded in the fight but the prince was victorious.

Agathos woke to hear the cries of his comrades and the terrifying shriek of the evil creature filling his tent. He had always expected such an attack, and his armour was ready beside his bed. He sprung to the ground and put it on. Then he fixed his sharp, bright sword to his side, bound the sandals upon his feet, and put his arm through the handle of his shield. Agathos was ready for battle.

At the door of his tent, he called upon the king's son for strength, then rushed forward. When the enemy saw him coming, he left off trampling upon the other soldiers and moved over to meet with this soldier in the king's armour.

Then there was a dreadful battle between the good soldier of the king and the king's fierce enemy. Agathos was beaten to his knees more than once. But the shield of faith protected him from the fiery darts which the evil one poured forth. Even as Agathos stumbled to the ground, new strength came to him.

Agathos was beaten to his knees more than once.

Quickly he regained his feet, and fought with a mighty strength against the merciless, destructive foe.

The battle was still raging when the sun went down. The good soldier was well nigh exhausted when he gathered all his available strength into one mighty blow. Calling aloud on the name of his prince, Agathos beat the creature of evil so fiercely that he fled away. The battlefield was silent.

Then Agathos was very glad, and he kneeled down to pray and give thanks and praise. Over the battlefield he could see the prince coming to him among the dew of evening. He heard his voice and he saw his face.

"Well done, good and faithful servant," said the prince. "Come with me to my father's home."

Agathos saw the wounds on the hands and feet of the prince, and he knew his dream had indeed been true.

"You are weary," continued the prince. "My father has a garden with a river as clear as crystal. Trees grow beside it and the leaves will heal and revive you. Come to the home which is now ready for you."

So Agathos was glad that he had remained faithful to the king: Ephesian 6:11-17 had been in the front of his mind always. Already the heat of the day and the fight with the evil enemy seemed as a fading dream. Soon he would meet with his king.

NOT LOST, BUT GONE BEFORE!
by Margaret Gatty

"I wonder what becomes of the frog when he climbs up out of this world and disappears, so that we do not see even his shadow; till, splash! he is among us again when we least expect him. Does anybody know where he goes to? Tell me, somebody, pray!"

Thus chattered the grub of a dragonfly as he darted about with his numerous companions, in and out among the plants at the bottom of the water, in search of prey.

The water formed a beautiful pond in the center of a wood. Stately trees grew around it and reflected themselves on its surface, as on a polished mirror. The bulrushes and forget-me-nots which fringed its sides, seemed to have a double existence, so perfect was their image below.

"Who cares what the frog does?" answered one of those who overheard the grub's inquiry. "What is it to us?"

"Look out for food for yourself," cried another, "and leave other people's business alone "

"But I have a curiosity about the subject," explained the first speaker. "I can see all of you when you pass by me among the plants in the water here. And when I don't see you any longer, I know you have gone on. But I followed a frog just now as he went upwards, and all at once he went to the side of the water, and then began to disappear, and presently he was gone. Did he leave this world, do you think? And what can there be beyond?"

"You idle, talkative fellow," cried another, shooting by as he spoke. "Attend to the world you are in, and leave the 'beyond'—if there *is* a 'beyond'—to those that are there. See what a meal you have missed with all your wonderings about nothing." So saying, the insolent speaker seized an insect which was flitting right in front of his friend.

The curiosity of the grub was a little checked by these and similar remarks, and he resumed his employment of chasing prey for a time.

But, do what he would, he could not help thinking of the curious disappearance of the frog, and presently began to trouble his neighbours about it again. *"What becomes of the frog when he leaves this world?"*

The minnows eyed him askance and passed on without speaking, for they knew no more than he did of the matter, but did not wish to show their ignorance. The eels wriggled away in the mud out of hearing, for they could not bear to be disturbed.

The grub grew impatient, but he succeeded in infecting several of his friends with some of his own curiosity, and then went scrambling about in all directions with his followers, asking the same unreasonable questions of all the creatures he met.

Suddenly there was a heavy splash in the water, and a large, yellow frog swam down to the bottom among the grubs.

"Ask the frog himself," suggested a minnow as he darted by overhead, with a mischievous glance of his eye.

And very good advice it seemed to be; only the thing was much easier said than done, for the frog was a dignified sort of person. The smaller inhabitants of the water stood a good deal in awe of him. It required a great amount of courage to ask a creature of his standing where he had been to, and where he had come from. He might justly consider such an inquiry a very impertinent piece of curiosity.

Still, such a chance of satifying himself was not to be lost, and after taking two or three turns round the roots of a waterlily, the grub screwed up his courage, and approaching the frog in the meekest manner he could assume, he asked, "Is it permitted for a very unhappy creature to speak?"

The frog turned his gold-edged eyes upon him in surprise, and answered, "Very unhappy creatures had better be silent. I never talk but when I am happy."

"But *I* shall be happy *if* I may talk," interposed the grub, as glibly as possible.

"Talk away, then," cried the frog. "What can it matter to me?"

"Respected frog," replied the grub, "but it is something I want to ask you."

"Ask away," exclaimed the frog—not in a very

encouraging tone but, still, the permission was given.

"What is there beyond the world?" inquired the grub, in a voice scarcely audible from emotion.

"What world do you mean?" replied the frog, rolling his goggle eyes round and round.

"This world, of course. *Our* world," answered the grub.

"This *pond,* you mean!" remarked the frog.

"I mean the place we *live* in, whatever you may choose to call it," cried the grub. *"I* call it the world."

"Do you, sharp little fellow?" rejoined the frog. "Then what is the place you *don't* live in, the 'beyond,' eh?"

And the frog shook his sides with merriment as he spoke.

"That is just what I want you to tell me," replied the grub briskly.

"Oh, indeed, little one!" exclaimed the frog, rolling his eyes this time with an amused twinkle. "Come, I shall tell you then. It is dry land."

There was a pause of several seconds, and then, "Can one swim about there?" inquired the grub in a subdued tone.

"I should think not," chuckled the frog. "Dry land is not water, little fellow. That is just what it is *not.*"

"But I want you to tell me what it *is,*" persisted the grub.

"Of all the inquisitive creatures I ever met, you certainly are the most troublesome," cried the frog. "Well, then, dry land is something like the sludge at the bottom of this pond, only it is not wet, because there is no water."

"Really!" interrupted the grub. "What is there, then?"

"That's the difficulty," exclaimed the frog. "There *is* something, of course, and they call it air. But I don't know how to explain it to you. My feeling about it is that it's the nearest possible approach to nothing. Do you comprehend?"

"Not quite," replied the grub, hesitating.

"Exactly. I was afraid not. Now just take my advice, and ask no more silly questions. No good can possibly come of it," urged the frog.

"Honoured frog," exclaimed the grub. "I must differ with you there. Great good will come of it, I think, if my restless curiosity can be satisfied by obtaining the knowledge I seek. If I learn to be contented where I am, it will be something. At present I am miserable and restless under my ignorance."

"You are a very silly fellow," cried the frog. "You will not be satisfied with the experience of others. I tell you the thing is not worth troubling yourself about. But, as I rather admire your spirit (which, for so insignificant a creature, is astonishing), I will make you an offer. If you choose to take a seat on my back, I will carry you up to dry land myself, and then you can judge for yourself what there is there and how you like it. I consider it a foolish experiment, mind, but that is your own look out. I make my offer simply to give you pleasure."

"And I accept it with a gratitude that knows no bounds," exclaimed the enthusiastic grub.

"Drop down on my back, then, and cling to me as well as you can. For, remember, if you go falling off, you may be lost when I leave the water."

The grub obeyed and the frog, swimming gently upwards, reached the bulrushes by the water's side.

"Hold fast," he cried and then, raising his head out of the pond, he clambered up the bank, and got upon the grass.

"Now, then, here we are," exclaimed he. "What do you think of dry land?"

But no one spoke in reply.

"Halloo! Gone?" he continued. "That's just what I was afraid of. He has floated off my back, stupid fellow. I declare! Dear, dear, how unlucky! But it cannot be helped. And perhaps he may make his way to the water's edge here after all, and then I can help him out. I will wait about and see."

And away went the frog, with an occasional jaunty leap along the grass by the edge of the pond, glancing every now and then among the bulrushes to see if he could spy the dark figure of the dragonfly grub.

But the grub, meanwhile? Ah, so far from having floated off the frog's back through carelessness, he had clung to it with hope, and the moment came when his face began to leave the water.

But that same moment sent him reeling back into the pond, panting and struggling for life. A shock struck his frame, and it was several seconds before he could recover himself.

"Horrible!" he cried, as soon as he had rallied a little. "Beyond this world there is nothing but death. The frog has deceived me. He cannot go *there,* at any rate."

With these words, the grub moved away to his old occupations, his excitement for knowledge grievously checked, though his spirit was unsubdued.

He contented himself, therefore, with talking to friends about what he had done and where he had been. And who could listen unmoved? The expectation, the mystery, the danger, the all-but-fatal result and the still unexplained wonder of what became of the frog—all invested the story with a romantic interest! The grub soon had a host of followers, questioning and chattering at his heels.

By this time the evening had come, and pursuit of prey was gradually becoming suspended. Then, as the inquisitive grub was returning from a ramble among the water plants he suddenly encountered, sitting silently on a stone at the bottom of the pond, his friend—the yellow frog.

"*You* here!" cried the grub. "You never left this world at all, I suppose! What a deception you must have practised upon me! This is what comes of trusting strangers, as I was foolish enough to do."

"You puzzle me by your offensive remarks," replied the frog, gravely. "Nevertheless, I forgive you, because you are so ignorant that civility cannot reasonably be expected from you, little fellow. It never struck you, I suppose, to think what *my* sensations were when I landed this morning on the grass, and discovered that you were no longer on my back. Why did you not sit fast as I told you? But this is always the way with you foolish fellows who think you can fathom and investigate everything. You are thrown over by the first practical difficulty you meet."

"Your accusations are full of injustice," exclaimed the indignant grub.

It was clear they were on the point of quarrelling, and would certainly have done so had not the frog, with unusual generosity, asked the grub to tell his own story and clear himself of the charge of clumsiness if he could.

It was soon told. The frog stared at him in silence out of those great, goggle eyes while the grub went through the details of his terrible adventure.

"And now," said the grub, in conclusion, "as it is clear that there is nothing beyond this world but death, all your stories of going there yourself must be mere inventions. So, if you do leave this world at all, you go to some other place you are unwilling to tell me of. You have a right to your secret, I admit. But, as I have no wish to be fooled by any more travellers' tales, I will bid you a very good evening."

"You will do no such thing, till you have listened as carefully to my story as I have done to yours," exclaimed the frog. Then he told how he had remained by the edge of the pond in the vain hope of seeing the grub, how he had hopped about in the grass, how he had peeped among the bulrushes. "And at last," he continued, "though I did not see you, I saw a sight which has more interest for you than for any other creature that lives." And there he paused.

"And what was that?" asked the inquisitive grub, his curiosity reviving.

"Up the polished green stalk of one of those bulrushes I beheld a grub just like you, slowly and gradually climbing till he had left the water behind him. He was clinging firmly to his chosen support, exposed to the full glare of the sun. Rather wondering at such a sight, considering the fondness you all show for the shady bottom of the pond, I continued to gaze, and observed presently that a break seemed to come in your friend's body. Gradually, by degrees, and after many struggles, there emerged from it one of those radiant creatures who float through the air. I spoke to you of them—they dazzle the eyes of all who catch glimpses of them as they pass. It had become a glorious dragonfly!

"Then he lifted his wings out of the casing which he was forsaking and, though shrivelled and damp at first, they stretched and expanded in the sunshine, till they glistened as if with fire." The frog closed his eyes as though seeing the sight again in his memory.

"How long the strange process continued I can scarcely tell, so fixed was I in astonishment and admiration. But I saw the beautiful creature at last poise for a second or two in the air before he took flight. I saw four long wings flash back the sunshine that was poured on them. I heard the clash with which

". . . after many struggles."

they struck the air and I beheld his body give out rays of glittering blue and green as he darted along. And away, away, over the water in eddying circles that seemed to know no end. Then I plunged below to seek you, rejoicing for your sake in the news I brought."

The frog stopped short and a long pause followed.

"It is a wonderful story," observed the grub at last, with less emotion than might have been expected.

"A wonderful story, indeed!" repeated the frog. "May I ask your opinion about it?"

"First tell me what *your* thoughts are upon the matter," was the grub's polite reply.

"Good! You are growing obliging, my little friend," remarked the frog. "Well then, I incline to the belief that what I have seen accounts for your otherwise unreasonable curiosity, your tiresome craving for information about the world beyond your own. That world will one day belong to you!"

"This is possible, provided your account can be depended upon," mused the grub, with a doubtful air.

"Little fellow," exclaimed the frog, "remember that your distrust cannot injure me. I know what I saw!"

"And you really think, then, that the glorious creature you describe was once a —"

"Silence!" cried the frog. "I am not prepared to discuss the matter further. Adieu! The shades of night are falling on your world down here. I return to my grassy home on dry land. Go to rest, little fellow, and awake in hope."

The frog swam close to the bank, and clambered up its side, while the grub returned to his tribe, which during the hours of darkness, rested from its life of activity and pursuit.

* * * * * *

"Promise!" uttered an entreating voice.

"I promise," was the earnest answer.

"Faithfully?" urged the first speaker.

"Solemnly," replied the second.

But the voice was languid and weak, for the dragonfly grub was sick and uneasy. His limbs had lost their old activity, and a strange feeling was coming upon him.

The creatures whom he had been accustomed to chase for food passed by him unharmed. The water plants over which he used to scramble with so much agility were now unpleasant to his feet. The very water itself into which he had been born now felt suffocating.

Upwards he must go now, upwards, upwards! This strong sensation now mastered every other, and to it he must submit as to some inevitable law. And then he thought of the frog's account and felt a trembling conviction that the time had come when the riddle of his own fate would be solved.

His friends and relations gathered around him. Some were his own age, and some were a generation younger, who had only that year entered upon existence. All of them were followers and friends whom he had inspired with his own enthusiastic hopes. If they could have, they would have helped him in this, his hour of weakness. There was no help for him now but hope. Hope he possessed, perhaps even more than they did.

Then came an earnest request, followed by a solemn promise that if the great hope proved true, he would return and tell them so.

"But if you should forget—!" exclaimed one of the younger generation, timid and uneasy.

"Forget the old home, my friend?" said the grub. "Forget our life of enjoyment here, the ardour of the chase, the triumph of success? Forget the emotions of hope and fear we have shared together? Impossible!"

"But you may not be able to come back to us," suggested another.

"More unlikely still," murmured the half-exhausted grub. "To a life so magnificent as the one in store for us, what can be impossible? Adieu, my friends, adieu! I can tarry here no longer. Before long you may expect to see me again in a new and more glorious form. Till then, farewell!"

Tired indeed was the voice, and slow were the movements of the grub as he rose up through the water to the reeds and bulrushes that fringed its bank. Two favourite brothers and a few of his friends, more adventurous than the rest, accompanied him in his ascent, in hope of witnessing whatever might take place above. But in this they were to be disappointed.

From the moment when, clinging with his feet to the stem of a bulrush, he emerged from his native element into the air, his companions saw him no more.

Eyes fitted only for the water were incapable of the

upward glance and power of vision which would have enabled them to pierce beyond it. The little group descended sorrowfully to the bed of the pond.

The sun was high in the heavens when the dragonfly grub departed from his friends, and they waited through the long hours of the day for his return—at first, in joyful hope, then in anxiety. As the shades of evening began to deepen around, they stood in gloomy fear that changed at last to despair.

"He has forgotten us," cried some.

"A death from which he never can awake has overtaken him," said others.

"He will return to us yet," maintained the few who clung to hope.

But in vain messenger after messenger shot upwards to the bulrushes and to various parts of the pond, hoping to discover some trace of the lost one. All who went out returned dispirited from the vain and weary search.

At last, night closed upon them, bringing a temporary suspension of grief. But the beams of the next rising sun, while it filled all nature beside with joy and hopefulness, awakened them to a sense of the bitterest disappointment. They had a feeling of indignation at the deception which had been practised upon them.

"We once managed very well without thinking of such things," they said. "But to have hopes like those held out, and to be deceived after all—it is more than we can be expected to bear!"

Then, with a fierceness which nothing could restrain, they hurried about in the destructive pursuit of prey, carrying a terrible vengeance in all directions.

And thus passed the hours of the second day, and before night a sort of grim and savage silence was agreed upon among them, and they ceased to bewail either the loss of him they had loved, or their own uncertain destiny.

But on the morning of the third day, one of the grub's favourite brothers silently came into the midst of a group who were just rousing up from rest, ready to recommence the daily business of their life.

There was an unnatural brilliance about his eyes, which shone as they had never done before. They startled all who looked at them.

"My friends," he said, "I was, as you know, one of our lost relative's favourite brothers. I trusted him, as if he had been a second self, and would have pledged myself a thousand times for his word. Judge, then, what I have suffered from his as yet unfulfilled promise. Alas, he has not yet returned to us!"

The favourite brother paused, and a group in a corner by themselves murmured among themselves, "How could he? The story about that other world is false!"

"He has not returned to us," repeated the favourite brother. "But, my friends, I feel that I am going to *him*—wherever that may be—to that new life he spoke about. Dear ones, I go, as he did, upwards, upwards, upwards! An irresistible desire compels me to it. But before I go, I renew to you—for myself and for him—the solemn promise he once made to you. Should the great hope be true, we will come back and tell you so. Rely on me; my word is more to me than life itself. Adieu!"

The grub rose upwards through the water followed by the last of the three brothers, and one or two of the younger ones. On reaching the brink of the pond he seized on a plant of the forget-me-not variety and, clinging to its firm flower stalk, clambered out of the water into the open air.

Those who accompanied him watched as he left the water. But after that they saw him no more. They sank down, sad and uneasy, to their home below.

The hours of the day passed on as before, and not a trace of the departed one was seen. In vain they held to the consoling words he had spoken. Their hope died with the setting sun, and many a voice was raised against his treachery and lack of love.

"He is faithless!" said some.

"He forgets us, just like his brother did," cried others.

"The story of that other world is false," muttered the group in the corner by themselves.

Only a very few murmured to each other, "We will not despair."

Another day now passed and then, in the early dawn following, the third and last brother crept slowly to a half-sleepy knot of his friends and roused them.

"Look at my eyes," he said. "Has a change come over them? To me, they feel swelled and bursting, and I see with a clouded and imperfect vision. Doubtless it is with me now, as it was with our dear ones before they left us. I am oppressed, like them. Like them, an invisible power is driving me upwards, as they were driven. Listen, then, for you may depend on my parting words. Let the other world be what it will—gorgeous beyond all we can imagine of it, blissful beyond all we can hope of it, you will not find in me a forgetful heart. If it be possible, I *will* return. But, remember, there may well be that other world and yet we, in ours, may misjudge its nature. Farewell, never part with hope!"

And he too went upwards through the cool water to the plants that bordered its side. Then, from the leaf of a golden king-cup he rose into the world of air, into which water-grub's eye never could pierce.

His companions lingered awhile near the spot where he had disappeared, but neither sign nor sound came to them. Only the dreary sense of bereavement reminded them that he had once been with them.

Then followed hours of waiting, renewed disappointment, cruel doubts, and hope mixed with despair. And after this others went upwards in succession. The time came to all when the lustrous eyes of the perfect creature shone through the masked face of the grub, and each felt compelled to pass upwards to the fulfillment of its destiny.

But, among those who were left, the result was always the same. There were always some who doubted and feared, some who disbelieved and ridiculed, and some who hoped and looked forward without fear.

Ah, if those eyes, fitted for the narrow limits of their water world, could have been given a power of vision into the purer element beyond, what a lifetime of anxiety many would have been spared! What peace, what joy could have been theirs!

And what of the dragonfly? Was he really faithless as they thought? When he burst from his prisonhouse by the waterside and rose on glittering wings into the summer air, had he indeed no memory for the ones he had so recently left behind? Had he no tender concern for their griefs and fears? No recollection of the promise he had made?

Far from it. He thought of them amidst the excitement of his wildest flights, and returned time and time again to the edge of that world which had once been the *only* world he knew. But now he could never return to the world of water.

The least touch upon its surface (as he skimmed over it with the intention of returning), brought on a deadly shock, like that which he had experienced as a water-grub, on emerging into air. His wings involuntarily bore him instantly back from the no longer natural contact with the water.

"Alas for the promise I made in ignorance and presumption, miserable grub that I was," was his constantly repeated cry.

And thus, divided and yet near, parted and yet united by love, he hovered about the barrier that lay between them, never without hope that some accident might bring his dear ones into sight.

Nor was his watchfulness unrewarded for, even after his longest roamings, he never failed to return to the old spot. He was there to welcome the brother who soon followed him.

And often, after that, the breezy air by the forest pond would resound in the bright summer afternoons with the clashing of dragonflies' wings as, now backwards, now forwards, now to one side, now to another, they darted over the crystal water in the rapture of their new life.

There were even happier times when some fresh arrival of friends or family members from below added an even greater joy to their already joyous existence. It was so assuredly sweet to each newcomer to find—not a strange and friendless abode—but a home rich with welcome from those who had gone before.

They darted over the crystal water.

THE SPRING MORNING
by Samuel Wilberforce

It was a beautiful morning in the large garden. Several children were at play. One group seemed happier than the rest. They were chasing and running through the shrubs and along the stream, following brightly coloured butterflies and laughing all the time.

At last they paused to rest by the stream where it ran through the bottom of the garden. They refreshed themselves with wild strawberries which grew on its banks. There were four children—two boys and two girls. All seemed about the same age.

Suddenly they looked up from their eating. A man had come through the trees that bordered the garden. He sat down in the shade and called the four children around him. They appeared to recognise him, for they did not approach him as they would approach a stranger.

"This," said the man quietly, "is the garden where I have put you all so that you can play. But it is not a place where you can stay for long."

The four looked puzzled. "But it is such a pleasant place that we do not wish to leave here," said one.

The man shook his head and smiled a sad smile. "To you it looks beautiful and safe. By evening this garden

. . . running along the stream . . .

will not be a safe place for you. If you play here until dark you will find that your games lose their pleasure. Then, when darkness falls, you will hear the roaring of many wild beasts around you. In the darkness you will see their eyes glaring out of the bushes. The birds and their cheerful songs will all be gone."

The four children shook their heads in disbelief. Surely this could not be true, they said to each other.

The man saw their faces and drew the four closer to him, and pointed into the distance. "You may stay here for a while, but remember that you must not make it your home. Your real home, which I have prepared for you, is in that direction. It is with my father, the king. But before you reach it, you have to pass over those hills and the hot places—some of which you will find dangerous. But you need have no fear of harm if you follow my instructions carefully. I have made the journey myself, and you will see my footprints all along the path. But more than this: I shall walk with each of you, although you will not see me."

One of the boys, named Edward, spoke now. "Can that new home really be better than *this?*"

"Not only better," replied the man, "but it will be your home forever. No danger can ever reach you there. There will be no darkness, neither will there be evil beasts to frighten or harm you. It is a home of love and peace and beauty."

Rachel said that she wanted to be the first to get there, so good did it sound. Charlotte and Oliver did not appear quite so certain.

"We shall all go together," exclaimed Edward. "How soon may we set out?" He, too, seemed to be impatient to commence the journey.

"To some, the journey is an easy one," explained the man. "But many travellers find it hard at times. Remember that I will help you all along the way. Some places are steep to climb, while others are gentle to your feet. You must not try to leave the path that I have made for you all. Come, Charlotte and Oliver, will you start on the journey?"

"We would rather wait until the afternoon," said Oliver, awkwardly. "There can be no hurry to leave. Will the journey be easier if we start out at once?"

The man said that many found it to be so. "The path is surest and safest in the morning. Will you not start out with your two friends?"

Charlotte picked another wild strawberry. "Oliver will stay with me," she explained. "There can be no hurry. The darkness you speak of is far away. It is a beautiful, spring morning and this garden is too beautiful to think of leaving yet."

"Then I cannot *make* you go," replied the man. "But, see, I have some gifts for you. Here is a reed flute. It is a small thing to look at, but do not despise it. It will be a great help. You can be sure that I am with you all the time, even though you do not see me. When you play a few notes on this reed flute, you will know for certain that I am close. The wild beasts along the way will flee when they hear its gentle notes. If you are lost or cannot make out the path clearly, the music will make my footprints show out for you to follow."

Then he showed them how to blow upon it and make music. The music, the man explained, was called Prayer.

"I have another gift for each of you," he continued. "I have a bottle of the clearest water. It is called the Living Water. It will give you strength for the journey. Remember that I am with you all the way."

Edward and Rachel were already on their feet to receive their gifts. Charlotte and Oliver remained on the ground a little longer. As the man faded from their sight a discussion broke out as to whether the man had ever come to them at all.

Then Edward blew gently on his reed flute. The music filled the garden and sounded even sweeter than the song of the birds which had been singing overhead. Rachel looked at him and smiled. Their journey from the garden must start at once. There was not a moment to lose in setting out for the new home which the king's son had prepared for them!

"We will soon catch up with you," called Charlotte, as the two prepared to leave. "Perhaps you will get tired from starting out too quickly. Perhaps we will reach the new home before you!" Then she laughed, and Oliver laughed with her.

"Not so," replied Edward. "The man said that it is easier to start out early than to delay. Now that I know there is a better place for us, I would get no pleasure from staying here a moment longer."

Then, taking their reed flutes and bottles of Living

Water, Edward and Rachel bid their friends goodbye, urging them to start as soon as possible.

Again, Charlotte and Oliver laughed at their two friends. Oliver began to pick up stones and throw them at the two who had been his friends before the man came to the garden.

"Be quick," urged Edward to Rachel. "The sun is already getting high over the hills. Soon we shall be out of reach of the stones." He could see that Rachel was frightened. "Wait, I will blow upon the reed flute," he said. So he blew softly, and they could hear the taunting voices of the other two no more. Soon they were out of reach of the stones.

So they walked on together, and talked about the things they might find ahead.

"I wonder how long the journey will take us," said Edward. "I long to get safely to its end."

"I cannot think of the *end*," replied Rachel. "We have only just set out, and to tell the truth, I am a little afraid of what lies before us."

"The new home must be a wonderful place if it is better than the garden we have just left," said Edward, thoughtfully.

"The king will be there," said Rachel, and the thought cheered her up. "But do you really believe his son is with us now?"

As they talked, they saw the gentle path they had been walking along was becoming dry and stony. A stile across the way led into a barren valley.

Rachel held back. "There are thorns there," she

said fearfully.

Edward paused. "No. There is a path through the valley, which I can see clearly."

"If it is all the same to you," replied Rachel, "I think I will turn back."

"But I am sure the king's son is with us," protested Edward. "It would be foolish to turn back now. Not only is he with us, but I can see his footprints in front. He promised he would stay with us all through our journey. Listen, I will play a few notes on my reed flute."

Rachel would not listen, neither to Edward nor to the music of the reed flute. But to Edward the way ahead did not seem even the slightest bit frightening now. He jumped over the stile lightly.

"Wait for me!" called Rachel.

"Then you must come quickly," replied Edward, who was already some way along the stony path.

"First I must pick some of this fruit," called Rachel. "We may not be able to find any along that path. It looks like it leads through such a desolate valley."

"You must not delay," urged Edward. "The king's son will provide enough food for us when we need it. If you stop to pick it now, you will slow both of us down."

"Then I shall only pick a little," agreed Rachel, but she stayed for a long time before crossing the stile.

"Why, how fast you are going," she complained to Edward once they had resumed their journey. "I am afraid I shall never be able to keep up with you. I think I shall rest here for a while. Charlotte and Oliver will soon catch up with us as they promised. Perhaps they will not be as eager to press forward as you are!"

Once more Edward begged his friend to come with him, and for a moment he almost succeeded. But try, as he most certainly did, Rachel could not be persuaded to continue with the journey for the time being.

"There will be time enough," she insisted. "Besides, the other two have probably not even started out yet. See, I have done better than they have by starting early with you. Go on now, and I will soon feel like continuing."

Before long, Rachel was alone. Edward, unable to convince his friend how important it was to keep on with the journey they had started, was soon out of sight down the valley.

It was not long before Rachel began to feel alone and frightened. So she crept back to the garden where Charlotte and Oliver were still resting by the bank of the stream.

"You're soon back!" called Oliver, as Rachel returned. Then he and Charlotte began to laugh as they thought of the hurry Rachel had been in to set off on her journey. But then Charlotte became silent, and wished deep down in her heart that she had set out with Edward, for she felt less inclined to go now than when the king's son had first spoken to them.

Then, as the sun rose higher in the sky, they all became good friends again and thought no more of Edward on his journey to the new home. By the middle of the day, when the sun was at its highest in the sky, the garden was too hot for play.

Charlotte began to think once again about Edward on his journey, and she wondered if the sun was as hot for him.

"Perhaps we should be setting out now," she said, half aloud.

Oliver heard her. "What, when the sun is so hot!" he jeered. "What stupid sort of person would set out on a journey when the sun is so high in the sky? No, there will be time enough for us all to start when the afternoon is cooler."

Charlotte sounded cross now. "I wish I had never stayed here, but had set out with Edward and Rachel! Why, where has Rachel gone?"

While the two of them had been arguing, Rachel had seen the king's son standing at the edge of the garden. She had looked down at her reed flute and felt a strong desire to play upon it. The sound of the music had not filled the garden, but the man had heard it and once again he told Rachel of the home that he had prepared for her. Gladly Rachel again had gone out on her journey, leaving her two quarreling friends behind.

Soon she came to the stile where she had left Edward. The path through the valley seemed more thorny and dangerous than ever now. The footprints Edward had seen were not clear to Rachel. The sun was very hot. There was not a breath of wind. Down through the long valley there were no trees for shelter. Edward would be far ahead. Rachel sat on the stile and began to cry.

Edward was indeed far ahead. At first, after leaving Rachel, he was sad and lonely. Then, as he played upon his reed flute, the certain feeling came over him that the king's son was with him just as he had promised. Then Edward thought of the king who would be waiting to welcome him to his new home. When he thought of this, even the hottest part of the valley did not seem unbearable.

Soon the path became green and easier. A stream, right alongside where Edward was walking, seemed even more pleasant than the stream in the garden he had left. At times the river must rise high after heavy rain, for there were dead leaves and branches caught above him on each side. Edward found he could walk along the large, flat stones in the bed of the river.

The path continued on the other side. The sun seemed to grow hotter and hotter in the sky, and suddenly Edward felt too tired to continue. Again, he pulled his reed flute from his pocket and played a gentle tune. Some bushes were ahead and they seemed an excellent place to provide shelter until the sun was lower in the sky.

As he reached the largest bush, dark and coolly inviting inside, Edward was aware of the king's son holding him gently but firmly by the shoulder. He pulled away almost angrily and would have sat down in the cool shade when he saw a snake watching him from under the low branches.

Edward drew back in alarm. "Perhaps, if I had fallen asleep there, I would never have woken up!" he

At times the river must rise high.

exclaimed to himself. "No, I will press on to the end of my journey. I can rest there, when I reach the beautiful new garden that has been prepared for me."

But as the sun scorched him, he thought of the bottle he had been given. He drank only a few drops of the Living Water but felt immediately refreshed and strengthened. It seemed as if the king's son spoke in his ear. "The sun shall not beat upon you unbearably by day, neither the moon by night."

Then, as Edward looked ahead, he saw that the path ran between the shelter of tall trees. How glad he was of the shade they gave him and of the cool breeze that blew between them. Now he could make his way along quickly and easily. Soon he was in a dark wood. All around him, among the trees, someone had set traps and snares.

"This would be a dangerous place to pass along in the twilight of evening," he said to himself, and immediately began to play upon his reed flute. Although he could not see the king's son, Edward knew that he was by his side.

A sudden noise among the trees caused Edward to stop in fright. In a moment a great lion appeared in front of him, ready to spring—its long, white teeth gnashing. The reed flute was already in Edward's hand. Loudly and urgently he played upon it, as his legs trembled in terror. At the first note the lion turned round and dashed into the undergrowth. Edward saw him no more. Instead of the angry growl, there came a voice with a refreshing breeze.

"Watch and pray," said the voice. "Resist the devil and he will flee from you."

Then Edward passed out of the wood, and before him in the distance he could see the gates of the beautiful garden, golden and shining. He would have run forward but his feet were weary, and it seemed there was still a long way to go. The sun beat down upon his head once again and seemed even hotter than before.

He wondered whether to return to the shelter of the wood, but as he played upon his reed flute the way ahead became easier and the sun became less hot. By the side of the road was a shelter built from leafy branches. In the king's writing, Edward saw a notice. It said that it was lawful for travellers to rest here awhile.

Being footsore and weary, Edward needed no further invitation. He sat down and drew out his bottle, and refreshed himself with the Living Water. His reed flute was always in his hand, and he played upon it softly. As he played, the sky clouded over and a mighty storm swept across the land. The rain fell in torrents and he could hear the wild beasts in the wood roaring their dreadful roars. But in his shelter Edward had no fear, for the man who had invited him to make the journey was there with him, although unseen. But Edward could feel his presence.

At last, the sky began to clear and Edward set out to continue on his way. The sun was now past its hottest place in the sky, and there was a cool breeze blowing on his face. He moved speedily on. It did not seem that it would be long now before he reached the golden gates of the garden where his new home would be.

Rachel had stayed by the stile for a long time. She could not bring herself to follow Edward until she realized that the sun was already moving round the sky. Much of the day had been wasted already—soon it might be too late to start! So, gathering up all her courage, Rachel climbed carefully over the stile onto the stony path.

Was it her imagination, or was the path really narrower than it had been when Edward had gone on ahead? It was certainly quite hard going for Rachel now. The thorns tore at her ankles, and for a moment she seemed inclined to return to the garden. Just then she remembered the reed flute which had been such a help to her friend. At first Rachel could not make it play any sort of tune, but the long, sad note that came from it was enough to let her know that the king's son was holding her hand and leading her carefuly along the path where it was safest to walk.

Rachel paused to pull the stopper from the bottle of the Living Water which she had been given earlier. At first she thought that the stopper would not yield but at last she was able to withdraw it. The Living Water gave her the strength to continue.

"Forgive me," she whispered. "Forgive me, for I have been very wrong."

Then came the quiet but definite voice that Edward had heard in the breeze. "You are not able to earn my forgiveness," the voice said. "You must accept it as a gift."

Rachel fell to the ground in dismay. "I will try harder to please you," she said.

"That is not what I want," said the voice. "Do you love the king?"

Rachel did not answer, but stood up and began to hurry on over the open ground. "I must show the king that I am determined to reach the new home which his son has prepared for me," she said to herself.

At that moment the storm, which had passed over the shelter where Edward had been resting, beat down upon the open ground where Rachel was now running. It beat upon her heavily. The rain fell in torrents, the fierce gusts of wind swept by her and the pealing thunderclouds seemed to come down all around.

The ground under Rachel's feet became miry with the rain, so that she slipped and fell as she tried to hurry for shelter. There was a hill in front and Rachel struggled to the top, for surely to press on like this would please the king.

Once over the hill, which provided no break from the storm, Rachel came to the stream that Edward had crossed so easily earlier in the day. Now it swelled into a roaring torrent and dashed along, foaming and boiling, carrying all along in its course.

Poor Rachel! What should she do? Either she must venture into the stream to reach the far bank, or else she must give up all idea of reaching the new home that was waiting for her.

The large rocks in the river were not fully covered by the water. So, plucking up a little courage, Rachel began to creep along them. First the water was ankle deep, then knee deep, then it rushed by her waist. Still she kept on, clinging tightly to the rocks. Another step and the water covered her shoulders and swept her feet from the ground.

Rachel clutched a rock, or she would have been carried away and drowned. She was not nearly through the stream—what if the next step should carry her away altogether?

The reed flute was in her dress pocket, although Rachel could have reached it easily if she had tried. But she thought only of reaching the far bank safely by her own strength. Each rock proved harder to reach than the last. The water seemed to grow colder.

Rachel could stand the force of the water no longer. Then it seemed to her that she could vaguely make out the form of the king's son standing right beside her in the fast-running torrent.

"My flute! my reed flute!" something seemed to say within her.

Caring nothing for her safety now, Rachel released her hold on the rock which she had been clinging to so desperately and reached for her flute. It seemed that even before she played it, she felt herself being lifted from the raging waters and placed gently on the grass of the bank.

"Forgive me," she said once again.

"It is a gift," said the voice. "You must accept it as a gift. You cannot reach the garden I have prepared for you unless you come to it my way. Your own strength

. . . she thought only of reaching the far bank safely.

will never get you to your new home with the king."

Rachel lay beside the river, exhausted. She felt that all her strength had gone, yet the voice spoke of her strength being too weak! She sighed in despair. Was there no way for her to complete her journey?

"You do not understand," continued the voice. "It is in your weakness that I want you to come and accept my forgiveness. I have told you that you are not able to earn it. Will you come?"

And, on the safety of the river bank, Rachel wept. For the first time since she had begun her journey she could see that the king's son loved her and wanted to forgive her. He wanted to forgive her not because she deserved it but simply because he wanted her to be with him in the safety of the new home which he had prepared for her.

Rachel slowly rose to her feet. "Forgive me. I *will* continue," she promised, "if you will come with me all along the way."

She could no longer see the man's form, but Rachel knew that he was there. It seemed to her that he was smiling and putting a caring arm around her shoulder.

"Have I not been with you always?" his voice seemed to say. "It was *you* who did not know that I was with you."

At this very moment Edward was reaching the golden gates. The sun had not quite set, and it hung over the top of the far hills and shone a red, golden brightness over everything. Rich and beautiful did those gates shine out before the glad eyes of the boy.

He could make out a crowd of heavenly forms within, wearing robes of light and crowns that looked like living fire.

And now, as he stood before the gates, his heart was full of hope and joy. Now, the troubles of the way were over. As he looked back over his shoulder at the path he had trodden, it seemed that all his difficulties had been no more than a preparation for this happy home.

He remembered the scorching sun no more. The weary hillside, the evil wood, the lion's fierce face, the storm; all these seemed to be as nothing compared to the splendid home that was awaiting him. His only thought was to thank the king and his son who had brought him safely through. As he lifted up his eyes to do so, he saw a sign over the gates, which said, "Knock, and it shall be opened."

Then Edward knocked with all his strength. As soon as he knocked, the golden gates began to open and he entered the garden.

Meanwhile, Rachel was entering the forest. As she came among the dark trees, the sun was setting over the far hills. The branches shut out all the light now, making the path impossible to see. But Rachel feared nothing. She played gently upon her reed flute and gained strength and courage from refreshing herself with the Living Water.

At times her feet tangled in the traps set by the side of the path, but they did not hold her for long. Then Rachel heard the dreadful roaring from the lion which had terrified Edward.

Throwing her reed flute to the ground in panic, Rachel began to run for the safety of the open ground which she could now see dimly in front. But it seemed that the king's son was holding her back, until she retrieved the instrument and played upon it once more. Then there was no need to run, for Rachel knew that she was now safe from all danger.

Once outside the wood, there was insufficient light to see the leafy shelter where Edward had rested during the storm. Indeed, there was no time to be lost in reaching her new home. Wearily Rachel pressed on, sometimes remembering to play upon her reed flute and, at other times, trying to get through the difficulties in her own way. But always the king's son walked with her.

At last she drew near the golden gates of the garden. The soft and gentle sounds of music from within gave her fresh hope. With a fast-beating heart, Rachel seized the golden knocker, and—Oh, joy of joys!—the gates opened for her entrance. Then poor, wavering Rachel, through the King's lovingkindness, entered the heavenly garden.

"Forgiveness is a gift," she murmured to herself as she entered. "It is a free gift!"

But what were Charlotte and Oliver doing at this time? Had they begun their journey? Perhaps they were to enter these golden gates soon.

After Rachel had slipped away from them to start once more upon her journey, Charlotte and Oliver sat awhile longer on the grassy bank beside the stream.

There was no need to run.

There seemed to be so little to do and, anyway, the sun was now hot in the sky. Charlotte fell asleep, and Oliver wandered slowly away, searching for fresh fruit from the trees across the garden.

The evening darkness came upon the garden suddenly. Oliver had been sitting with the fruit which he had picked, throwing stones. The first sign of danger came without warning. The growl of some large and savage beast frightened him, and he looked round for Charlotte. She was still sleeping upon the grassy bank.

The reed flute fell out of Oliver's pocket and he would have picked it up but the beast was now so close. It seemed to him that the flute would be of little use to him against this danger. Far better, he decided, to use his own fast legs and run from the garden. Was there not a path to the new home? If he tried hard enough, could he not get there in time? He was proud of his own strength!

Charlotte woke suddenly. The garden was silent. Surely she had heard a cry. Oliver had gone. Darkness was all around her. As she stood up, Charlotte noticed that the flute had fallen from her dress pocket while she had been sleeping. It was bent and damaged, and she doubted if it would play music any more.

Then, as Charlotte placed it to her lips, the king's son appeared before her. "You must take me from here," she begged, in tears. "It is only you who can save me now. Take me to the new home you have prepared for me." And she begged for forgiveness, which was freely given.

Then the man lifted Charlotte upon his strong shoulders and carried her safely through the raging torrent and the dark wood. For her, too, the golden gates swung open as she was brought into the heavenly home.

Edward and Rachel came forward to greet her, and they exchanged stories of their journeys. Charlotte began to cry.

"Whatever is the matter?" asked Rachel. "This new home is the happiest place there could ever be."

"But you deserve to be here," said Charlotte. "I am only here because the king's son carried me here in love."

Edward smiled. "There is *not one* person here who deserves this beautiful home. It is not a reward but a gift. We will go and meet the king. He will receive you because his son brought you here, as he brought us all here. Without him, we could not have made the journey."

"Come," said the king as they came before him, surrounded with a feeling of perfect love. "Come, Charlotte, I will dry your tears. Come, all of you."

And the three children stepped forward.

THE ROCKY ISLAND
by Samuel Wilberforce

I saw in a dream a rough and rocky island rising straight up from a roaring sea. In the middle of the island rose a steep, black mountain. Dark clouds hid the top of this mountain from sight but deep, red flames like a volcano lit up the black clouds from time to time. Angry lightning and thunder tore at the few trees that grew on the mountain, and sometimes one would be broken into pieces and would crash down into the sea.

My first thoughts were that the island was completely deserted, for who would want to live on such a wild and frightening place? Then, to my surprise, I saw that there was a beach covered with soft, white sand, and on this beach there were children at play. Many of them were running here and there. Some were collecting shells, others were picking bright orange berries from bushes that grew by the cliffs. A few raced towards the water in fun, and then ran back quickly as the waves rushed up the sands towards them.

A child was calling to the seabirds to come. They stood watching as the child crept close, holding out a hand. The birds hopped away, but did not appear to feel themselves in any danger. A loud roar from the top

Dark clouds hid the top . . .

of the mountain sent deep, red flames into the black clouds that enveloped its top, and I was surprised how little concern the children seemed to have for the dangers that surrounded them.

As the roar from the mountain got louder, they paused in their play. The thunder crashed closer than ever, making everyone run together in a frightened group. Soon the thunder died away, and before long all was forgotten, and the children started to play their games once more.

For some time I stood and watched. Then to my surprise a man appeared. He walked slowly along the beach, calling to the children to gather round him. He seemed a noble man, like a king, yet the children were not afraid to come close. His face was kind, and his voice gentle.

"Listen to me, children," I heard him say. "You will all certainly be killed if you stay on this rocky island. You cannot go on playing safely forever. I have come to show you the way to a safer and happier place. Believe me, you must not remain here any longer."

The children listened to the man quietly, and then turned to each other.

"How can we get away?" I heard one child whisper to another. "We will never be able to swim across the sea. I believe we ought to stay here and risk the dangers of the mountain."

The man heard what was whispered. He put a kind arm around the child. "Do not stay here," he warned in a firm but gentle voice. "You certainly cannot swim to safety. There is no way you can get away by yourselves, but I have made a way of escape. Follow me and you will see."

Then the man led the children round a high rock to another beach. Here the sea was calm, and rippled among a fleet of small, brightly coloured sailing boats. Each boat was just large enough for one person. There was a rudder to steer with, a pure, white sail to carry the boat along its course and, at the top of each mast, a white flag with a cross of bright red. The flag and the sail fluttered gently in the breeze.

When the children saw these boats they clapped their hands in excitement. But the man held out a hand in warning. "The voyage is going to be difficult, and the sea is stormy and dangerous. These boats will carry you over it in absolute safety but only if you do as I say. The waves may be high and frightening at times, but these boats are going to take you to a bright and beautiful land where there is no angry mountain. There will be trees by the side of a beautiful river. The trees will always be green, and the leaves always fresh. The fruits on the trees will ripen every month and the leaves of the trees will heal you. There is always happiness and light there."

The man paused and smiled a reassuring smile at the children who were listening so closely. "There are others there who have passed safely over this sea. Some of you will find fathers and mothers, and brothers and sisters. I shall look after you and be with you always."

As soon as the man had finished speaking, the children were all anxious to jump into a boat and be on their way. The man helped them in. He spoke to each child, and promised to help them on their way. They must never look back at this island which they were leaving. They must always keep their eyes open for the happy land they were setting out for. If they had any shells or berries with them, they must leave them behind. If they tried to take these with them in the boats, they would soon be in difficulty.

When some of the children heard this, they crept secretly away, and ran back around the large rock to the beach where they had been playing. Then, to my surprise, I thought I could see some of the others hiding shells and berries in their pockets, and then jumping into their boats, pretending they had left all behind.

The man had presents for the children in the boats. There was a compass in a wooden box. "You will each have one of these," said the man, "and you will know the way to steer. You are to follow me, for I will always be leading the way across the water. I have called this compass Bible, for often—when the darkness of night comes on or a thick mist surrounds you or there is no breeze to help you on your way—you may not be able to see me. It is then that you must look at the compass, and its finger will always point true and straight to where I am."

There was another present for each child, a musical instrument that gave out a soft, murmuring sound when blown into very hard. "I have called this Prayer," said the man. "You can use it as often as you wish. It will help the voyage pass easily. Use it also when your boat will not keep on course, or when the waves are large and frightening. And here is some bread and water which will last all through the voyage."

As the boats sailed away from the rocky island, I thought how beautiful they all looked. Their snow-white sails stood out against the dark blue of the sea. They looked like bright stars in a dark, night sky. The leader's boat moved slowly and they all followed closely. So far, all the children seemed to be finding the voyage easy.

Then, as I watched, I could see some of the boats were dropping behind, although most of them still followed closely behind the leader. A few were even going way off to the right or left.

At first I was puzzled that they should be drifting away so soon. Then I could see that there were many different reasons for this. In one boat, the child kept turning back to look at the island that had been his home. He seemed to have forgotten the man's warning. While he kept turning to look, his boat drifted further and further back, towards the rocky island. Then the sound of the children who had been left behind came clearly across the waves. They seemed to be having such fun that the boy forgot the burning mountain and the dangers. He forgot the bright and happy land he had been so excited to set course for in the boat. He forgot the kind and gentle person who had promised to help him through all difficulties. As he listened to the

Their . . . sails stood out against the dark blue of the sea.

others playing, a wave lifted his boat and carried it roughly onto the rocks that were close to the beach.

I turned in disappointment and saw two other boats, which were keeping close together but for some reason going faster and faster away from the true course. Then I saw that the two children were having a race with each other, but they were very angry. They were so busy trying to get the better of each other that they forgot to look for their leader's boat, or to watch the finger of the compass. The more they tried to race each other, the further they went in the wrong direction.

There was another boat which was also going in the wrong direction. This time there was no one at the rudder to steer the right course. The child was playing with something in the bottom of the boat. Then I saw he had some of the bright orange berries all the children had been warned to leave behind.

How foolish the child had been. As I watched, the boat was carried onto a hidden rock with such a force that a hole was ripped in its side, and it began to sink.

I turned away, sadly. Surely the boats that were following their leader closely would make me happier to watch. Here I was puzzled by the way the sea appeared. One boat would be sailing well in calm water while, close by, another would be battling through a sudden storm. One boat I saw was surrounded by a heavy darkness. The child called out to his friends, and when he heard them answer I knew that he was helped. But sometimes the darkness was too much to call through, and several boats were lost in silence.

In spite of the darkness, the child had only to look at his or her compass and the needle would light up to show the way. And then the child would blow on the musical instrument called Prayer, and the darkness lifted as the sweet music rose softly from the little boat. At times like this I thought the child could see more of the land their leader had told them of than could other children sailing close by.

Then I saw another boat that seemed to have stopped moving altogether. The boat and its sail were so still they could have been part of a painted picture. The wind and the waves had gone. It was strange that, close by, another boat shot along, its sail blowing out full in a fresh breeze. But the boat that lay in the calm water showed no sign of movement.

I saw this happen to many boats along the way. If the child sat in the bottom of the boat and did nothing, or perhaps played a game or two, the boat lay still until night came. However, if the child picked up the musical instrument and blew hard into it, the soft music seemed to whisper to the wind, and suddenly the blood-red cross of the flag would lift itself over the water and the sail would fill with a fresh breeze. Before long the boat would be dancing on its way.

I watched other boats that were going well, but would suddenly come to a dark and stormy patch of water. Great waves seemed to lift up their angry, white heads, but to each side the sea was calm. Quickly a child would look ahead for signs of his leader, or get out the compass. If the way led through stormy water, the child would need a bold heart and a faithful hand to steer straight ahead. But always, just when the water seemed to be most dangerous, the waves would die down and let the boat pass through in safety. Then the wind would blow the boat faster than ever before to the distant land.

How different for the child who decided not to trust the compass but to steer to the side, towards the calmer water. One or two children I was watching did this. One child had been getting on very well until now, but the sight of the raging waves frightened him very much. For a moment the boat kept straight ahead, but then turned at the last moment as the child steered into the calm. Then, when all seemed to be well after all, a hidden sand bank caught the boat and held it fast.

Another child followed this boat. This seemed to happen often. Whenever one boat went astray, another would follow it, the child quite forgetting to watch the compass called Bible and test the way. And so it happened now. The child who was following saw the sand bank in time and then tried to steer aside, but the water became deep and rough and tipped the little boat onto its side.

I was glad to see three or four boats getting along well together. Ever since they had left the rocky island they had stayed with each other. Few others had got on so well in their voyage. I could see, as I looked closely at their faces, that they were all children of one family. All through the voyage they were cheering each other up and helping first one and then another through difficulties. If one of them got into some sort of trouble with the boat, the others would come over to help. Instead of being slowed down by this, they seemd to get along faster and easier on their journey.

Now I longed to see how each voyage would end. So I stayed with the boat that was furthest forward, so I could see it come to land at last.

First this boat, and then the ones that followed, came to an area of storm and darkness just before the shore of the happy land. True, some of the boats found the storms and the darkness greater than did others. But every boat had to pass through this part of the sea. I saw too that each boat had to be parted from the others. Even those children who had been so close to each other had to separate when they reached this dark part. Each child had to go through it alone.

"When you go through deep waters and great trouble, I will be with you," called a voice.

The boats that sailed in fastest seemed to get through the best. Indeed, this happened every time. When the sailor kept an eye on the compass and held tight to the rudder, the storm and darkness did not trouble him. Another child would play soft music and eat the bread and water as he passed through, easily and swiftly. And I knew that this final storm and darkness were called Dying, and each child had to go through it to reach the happy land.

The Lord of these seas seemed to lighten the darkness with his face of beaming love. He seemed nearer now than at any other time during the voyage.

Then the boat would break through into the brightness of the beautiful land that lay beyond. The happy sound of friends, gathered on the shore to greet them, drifted across the water.

There were others there, too, who were like people, and yet they were different—such as children's eyes had only seen in some pleasant dream of angels. These were their friends, too, for they waited for the children on the beautiful shore. Then each child was lifted up and carried with songs of triumph into the shining presence of the merciful king.

There, on the royal throne, and with the glorious crown upon his head, each child saw the same kind face of gentle majesty which had looked upon them when they had played on the shore of that now distant rocky island. They heard the voice which had urged them to flee from the burning mountain.

The children looked up at the face of the man who had given them each a boat and told them to follow him. They saw the man who had been near them in the storm, who had given them light in the darkness and who had helped them through the times when their boats had been halted by the calm. They saw the Lord who had never left them, who had kept and guided them across the ocean—through the final storm and darkness—and who now received them to his never-ending rest.

"I am the one who raises the dead and gives them life again," said the king. "Anyone who believes in me, even though he dies like anyone else, shall live again.

He will be given eternal life for believing in me, and shall never perish" (see John 11:25).

Thrills! Action! Suspense! Drama!

Christiana's Journey The vivid account of a young girl's perilous journey. Fraught with unexpected danger, the road she travels is extremely difficult. Illustrates fortitude, perseverance and Christian principles.
P533-4 Trade Paper
ISBN 0-88270-533-4/U.S. Price $4.95

Young Christian's Pilgrimage *Pilgrim's Progress* made alive for young readers. The adventures of young Christian as he battles the dragon-like Appolyon, the Giant Despair, the Wicked Prince and other formidable foes. Children will read this book again and again—right to the last thrilling page!
P534-2 Trade Paper
ISBN 0-88270-534-2/U.S. Price $4.95

Christie's Old Organ A young boy finds life's greatest discovery! This classic story has been a favorite with generations of children. Poignant, charming and captivating!
P532-6 Trade Paper
ISBN 0-88270-532-6/U.S. Price $4.95

Target Earth! John Bunyan's *The Holy War* revised and updated for the 1980s! Follow the adventures of Keerdy and Temar—two angels sent on a mission to earth with a message from God to mankind! But tremendous obstacles stand in their path—will they get through in time?
P536-9
ISBN 0-88270-536-9/U.S. Price $4.95

A Peep Behind the Scenes Mrs. O.F. Walton's touching tale of God's love revealed in hard times and to callous, unloving people.
P538-5
ISBN 0-88270-538-5/U.S. Price $4.95

The Rocky Island and Other Stories Seven classic allegories for children.
P543-1
ISBN 0-88270-543-1/U.S. Price $4.95

**Revised and updated specially for the 1980s
by popular children's author Christopher Wright**

Our exciting new series of Victorian classics for children!

**Bridge Publishing, Inc.
South Plainfield, New Jersey 07080**

Order through your bookstore today!